Printed in China

First Edition
1 3 5 7 9 10 8 6 4 2

T425-2382-5-12294
ISBN 978-1-4231-7956-6

For more Disney Press fun, visit www.disneybooks.com
This book was printed on paper created from a sustainable source.

DISNEY·PIXAR
MONSTERS, INC.

Boo on the Loose

By Gail Herman
Illustrated by the Disney Storybook Artists

DISNEY PRESS

New York

James P. Sullivan was the top Scarer at Monsters, Inc. Scaring kids was an important job! Kids' screams kept the whole city running.

One day as Sulley was heading home, he noticed a door on the Scare Floor.

"Is anybody there?" he said.
Sulley peeked through the door.

"Boo!" something said. It was a little girl—inside the monster world! She had snuck through the open door.

"Aaah!" Sulley screamed. Children were like poison to monsters. Every monster knew that.

Sulley tried to put the girl back in her room, but she kept popping out!

Sulley had to do something. If anyone found out about her, he could lose his job!

There was only one monster Sulley could tell his secret to—his best friend, Mike. So Sulley hid the little girl in his bag and brought her home.

Mike could not believe it! A kid? In their world?
"Her name is Boo," said Sulley.
"You named it?" cried Mike.

They had to get rid of the little girl. So Mike came
up with a plan. The next morning, they would drive
her to the park and try to lose her.

The next morning, Sulley and Mike made a monster costume for Boo. Then they walked outside to Mike's car. "Be careful!" said Mike. "Don't let that kid touch anything!"

When they got to the park, Sulley and Mike got out of the car. Mike went to open the door, but Boo had locked herself in!

"We have to get her out!" Mike shouted.

Sulley had an idea. He opened the trunk and pulled out a spare tire. "Time to play!" he said.

Sulley put Mike in the middle of the tire and rolled him down a hill.

"Fun!" Sulley said.

"Yeah, fun," Mike grumbled.

But Boo did not get out of the car.

Next Sulley took out the car jack. He cranked Mike up and down. Boo still did not come out. She was too busy playing with Mike's bear.

Then Sulley swung Mike around.
"Don't you want to play, Boo?" Sulley asked.

But Boo just waved from inside the car. "What do we do now?" Mike shouted.

Just then, a monster butterfly flew past the car window. Boo smiled and pointed. Then she opened the car door and ran after it!

The butterfly flew to a fountain. Boo tried to catch it, but the butterfly was too fast. It flew into the woods, and Boo followed.

Mike grabbed Sulley's arm. "This is our chance, Sulley!" he shouted "Let's go!"

Sulley wasn't listening. He was thinking about Boo. He missed her already.

Mike tried to start the engine, but the car wouldn't start. "We're out of gas!" Mike said.

"We need to find Boo!" Sulley said. "Her scream will start the car."

Sulley ran into the woods.

"Boo?" Sulley called. "I have your teddy bear. . . ."

"Kitty?" said a small voice.
"Hi, Boo," Sulley said.
Boo hugged Sulley's leg.
Sulley smiled.
Boo did not seem dangerous at all.

Sulley walked back to the car.
"You're holding its hand!" Mike cried.
Sulley smiled. "I know," he said. "I feel okay, though."

Sulley helped Boo into the car. Then he got in, too.
"Now we need a scream," said Mike.

"Okay, Sulley," Mike said. "You're the best Scarer at Monsters, Inc. Do your stuff!"

Sulley looked at Boo. He opened his mouth to roar . . . but he couldn't do it. He just could not scare little Boo!

"Just scare it, NOW!" yelled Mike. He banged his head on the steering wheel. HONK! went the horn.

"Ouch!" Mike said. Boo laughed.

The engine started with a roar!

Mike looked at Boo. "Okay, she can stay for now," he said.

"But just remember, that is my bear!"